GUILTY

UNTIL PROVEN INNOCENT?

NARENDER SINGH

BlueRose ONE.com
Stories Matter
NewDelhi • London

BLUEROSE PUBLISHERS
India | U.K.

BlueRose ONE
Stories Matter
NewDelhi • London

For permissions requests or inquiries regarding this publication, please contact:

BLUEROSE PUBLISHERS
www.BlueRoseONE.com
info@bluerosepublishers.com
+91 8882 898 898
+4407342408967

ISBN: 978-93-7018-587-6

Cover Design: Aman Sharma
Typesetting: Pooja Sharma

First Edition: March 2025

Guilty Until Proven Innocent?

- A twist on the presumption of innocence, as the NCB pursues a law student.

Narender Singh

Preface

The law is a double-edged sword–it protects, but it also punishes. This book explores the fine line between knowing the law and bending it to one's advantage.

"Guilty Until Proven Innocent?", follows the journey of a law student who, despite his academic brilliance, finds himself entangled in a high-stakes game with the NCB. It is a story of ambition, morality, and survival in the face of legal scrutiny.

As a legal professional, I have witnessed firsthand how the justice system operates–not just in courtrooms but in the minds of those navigating it. This book is not just a crime thriller but a reflection of the complexities of law, the loopholes that exist, and the choices people make when caught between the system and the streets.

Through this fictional story of a law student about his life at law school, I invite readers to step into the world of law students, where textbooks teach one version of justice, but reality tells another.

Acknowledgments

Writing this book has been an exhilarating experience, and I owe my gratitude to several people who made it possible.

First and foremost, I thank Jayam Singh Chauhan, whose time I borrowed (and sometimes stole) to bring this story to life. Her patience and understanding during the countless meetings I cancelled to complete this work of fiction mean the world to me.

To my mentors and colleagues in the legal profession, whose insights into criminal law shaped my understanding of how cases unfold beyond textbooks–thank you for inspiring the realism in this narrative. To my friends and peers, who shared their own law school experiences, your stories added depth and authenticity to this tale.

A special thank you to my family, who have always supported my passion for storytelling, and to my readers, who bring life to these pages. Lastly, to every law student out there navigating the maze of legal studies–this book is for you.

About the Author

Narender Singh is a criminal defence lawyer practicing at the Delhi District and High Court, specializing in high-stakes cases under UAPA, MCOCA, NDPS,

and other complex criminal laws. With extensive experience of contesting cases against sophisticated agencies like the NIA, NCB, CBI, and Special Cell, he

brings a wealth of real-world insight to his writing.

An alumnus of the Faculty of Law, University of Delhi, Narender has always been fascinated by the intersection of legal theory and courtroom realities. His firsthand experiences in courtrooms, prisons, and dealing with investigative

agencies have shaped his unique perspective on justice.

"Guilty Until Proven Innocent?" is his debut novel, a gripping blend of legal drama and the thrilling intricacies of criminal investigations, inspired by his years in the trenches of the legal profession

Legal Disclaimer

This book is a work of fiction. Names, characters, places, and events are either the product of the author's imagination or used fictitiously. Any resemblance to actual persons, living or dead, events, or locations is purely coincidental.

The legal scenarios and procedures depicted in this book are based on general legal knowledge and do not constitute legal advice. Readers are advised to consult a professional for legal inquiries. The book does not promote or glorify illegal activities and is intended solely for entertainment and thought-provoking discourse.

Contents

Contents

Chapter 1: The First Step into a New World

The bus stopped smoothly, its doors opening with a soft hiss. Jinender Pratap Singh stepped off, his backpack hanging from one shoulder, and paused to steady himself on the busy Delhi sidewalk. Ahead, the Faculty of Law, University of Delhi, stood tall and impressive, its red- brick walls shining in the morning sunlight. Jinender adjusted his glasses and smiled slightly. He had done it—he was here.

The past year had been a whirlwind of late-night study sessions, mock tests, and endless revisions. But it had all paid off. The admission letter in his bag was proof of that. His parents had been thrilled when the news came.

Jinender took a deep breath, the energy of the campus already buzzing around him. Students hurried past, some in groups, others alone, all seemingly carrying the same mix of excitement and nervousness. He straightened his shirt—a crisp white one his mother had ironed to perfection—and tightened the strap of his backpack. This was it. The start of something new.

The Faculty of Law wasn't just any institution; it was a place where legends were made. Jinender had read about the alumni—judges, lawyers, policymakers—who had walked these very halls. He felt a surge of pride knowing he was now part of that legacy.

As he walked through the gates, he couldn't help but notice the vibrant, almost electric atmosphere of North Campus. Posters and banners adorned the walls, each one a bold declaration of political ideologies, student union campaigns, and calls for social justice. A group of students stood near the entrance, passionately debating something about policy reforms, their voices rising and falling like waves. Another group nearby was distributing pamphlets for an upcoming protest, their faces lit with determination.

Jinender paused for a moment, taking it all in. This was the heart of student politics in Delhi—a melting pot of ideas, ideologies, and activism. He had heard stories about the heated debates, the protests, and the sheer energy of North Campus, but seeing it firsthand was something else entirely.

He noticed the diversity around him—students from different states, speaking different languages, all united by a common goal. Some wore kurtas and scarves, others jeans and T- shirts with slogans emblazoned across them. It was inspiring, and Jinender felt a quiet determination settle over him. He was here to learn, to grow, and to make his mark.

The admission process had been tough, but Jinender had held his own. The written exam had been challenging, and the interview had tested his confidence, but he had stayed focused. His father's steady encouragement and his mother's quiet support had kept him going. They weren't wealthy, but they had given him everything he needed to succeed.

Jinender glanced at the noticeboard near the entrance, scanning the map for directions to the orientation hall. He didn't want to be late on his first day. As he walked, he took in the sights—the sprawling lawns, the ancient trees, the students lounging on the steps with books in hand. It was everything he had imagined and more.

The orientation hall was already filling up when he arrived. Jinender found a seat near the middle, his eyes darting around the room. The atmosphere was electric, a mix of anticipation and curiosity. A professor stepped onto the stage, and the room fell silent.

“Welcome to the Faculty of Law,” the professor began, his voice calm but commanding. “You are here because you have proven yourselves capable. But remember, this is just the beginning. The journey ahead will challenge you, push you, and shape you into the professionals you aspire to be.”

Jinender listened intently, his mind racing with possibilities. He thought of the years ahead– the lectures, the debates, the internships. He thought of the friends he would make, the mentors who would guide him, and the experiences that would shape his future.

When the orientation ended, Jinender lingered for a moment, taking it all in. He felt a sense of pride, but also a quiet resolve. He knew the road ahead wouldn’t be easy, but he was ready for it.

As he stepped back out into the sunlight, he felt a surge of energy. This was his moment. His first step into a world of endless possibilities.

The journey had just begun, and Jinender Pratap Singh was ready to make it count.

Chapter 2:
New Beginnings and New Bonds

The first week of classes at the Faculty of Law flew by in a blur of introductions, syllabi, and the occasional awkward silence in lecture halls. Jinender Pratap Singh found himself settling into a rhythm, his initial nervousness giving way to a quiet confidence. The campus was everything he had imagined–vibrant, chaotic, and alive with energy. But what surprised him most were the people he was beginning to meet.

It started in his first Criminal Law lecture. Jinender had taken a seat near the middle of the hall, his notebook open and pen ready. The professor, a stern but engaging woman with a reputation for being tough, had just begun her lecture when a voice whispered from beside him.

"Hey, do you have an extra pen? Mine just died."

Jinender turned to see a tall, lanky guy with a mop of curly hair and a sheepish grin. He handed over a spare pen without a word, and the guy nodded in thanks.

"I'm Rohan," he said, scribbling his name on the corner of his notebook. "Rohan Mishra. From Lucknow."

"Jinender," he replied, smiling. "Jinender Pratap Singh. From Haryana."

Rohan's eyes lit up. "Haryana, huh? That's cool. I've heard people from there are tough as nails."

Jinender chuckled. "We try to be."

As the lecture progressed, Jinender learned that Rohan came from a modest background in Uttar Pradesh. His father was a schoolteacher, and his mother worked as a seamstress. Rohan had worked tirelessly to secure his place at the Faculty of Law, and his determination was evident in the way he hung on every word the professor said.

By the end of the class, Jinender and Rohan had exchanged numbers and made plans to meet for chai at the campus canteen later that day.

The canteen was buzzing with activity when Jinender and Rohan arrived. They found a table near the corner, where a girl with sharp features and a confident demeanour was already seated, flipping through a thick law textbook. She looked up as they approached.

"Mind if we join?" Rohan asked, gesturing to the empty chairs.

"Go ahead," she said, her voice carrying a slight accent that Jinender couldn't quite place. "I'm Jia. Jia Khongwir. From Shillong."

"Meghalaya?" Jinender asked, impressed.

Jia nodded, a small smile playing on her lips. "Yeah. First time in Delhi. It's... different." Jinender chuckled. "That's one way to put it."

Jia was sharp, witty, and unapologetically herself. She grew up in a small town in Meghalaya and had fought against societal expectations to pursue law. Her dream was to work in human rights, and her passion for justice was evident in the way she spoke.

As the three of them chatted, a fourth figure approached the table. He was dressed impeccably–crisp white shirt, tailored trousers, and a leather satchel that looked like it cost more than Jinender's entire wardrobe.

"Mind if I join?" he asked, though he was already pulling out a chair. "Sure," Jia said, raising an eyebrow. "And you are?"

"Aryan Kapoor," he said, flashing a confident smile. "Delhi boy, born and raised. My dad's a lawyer–senior advocate, actually. Guess you could say law runs in the family."

Jinender exchanged a glance with Rohan, who rolled his eyes slightly. Aryan's confidence bordered on arrogance, but there was something likable about him.

Over the next few days, the four of them–Jinender, Rohan, Jia , and Aryan–found themselves gravitating toward each other. They were an unlikely group, each coming from vastly different backgrounds, but they shared a common drive to succeed.

Rohan was the quiet, hardworking one, always scribbling notes and asking thoughtful questions in class. Jia was the fiery, outspoken one, unafraid to challenge professors or classmates when she disagreed. Aryan was the smooth talker, his confidence masking a surprisingly sharp legal mind. And Jinender? He was the observer, the one who listened more than he spoke but always had something insightful to add.

One evening, as they sat on the steps of the Faculty building, watching the sun set over the campus, Aryan turned to the group.

“You know,” he said, “we’re going to be legends one day. Just wait and see.” Jia laughed. “Legends? Speak for yourself, Kapoor.”

“No, seriously,” Aryan insisted. “Think about it. Rohan’s going to be the judge, Jia ’s going to be the human rights activist, Jinender’s going to be the criminal defence lawyer, and I’m going to be the suave corporate lawyer making millions.”

Jinender smiled, shaking his head. “We’ve got a long way to go before any of that happens.” “True,” Rohan said, leaning back on his elbows. “But it’s not a bad dream to have.”

As the sky turned shades of orange and pink, Jinender felt a sense of belonging he hadn’t expected. He had come to the Faculty of Law to study, to learn, to build a future. But he was starting to realize that the people he met along the way might just be the most important part of the journey.

And so, with his new friends by his side, Jinender Pratap Singh took another step forward into the world of law, ready to face whatever challenges lay ahead.

Chapter 3: The Allure of the Unfamiliar

The hostel courtyard was alive with energy, the sound of laughter and music spilling out into the cool night air. Jinender Pratap Singh stood near the edge of the crowd, clutching a paper cup of soda, feeling both out of place and oddly exhilarated. He had never been to a college party before, let alone one hosted by seniors. Back in Haryana, his life had been predictable– early mornings, long study hours, and the occasional cricket match with friends. But here, in the heart of Delhi University's North Campus, everything felt different.

The party had been Rohan's idea. "Come on, Jinender," he had said earlier that evening, tugging at his arm. "You can't spend your entire college life buried in books. Let's see what the seniors are up to."

Reluctantly, Jinender agreed. Now, as he watched groups of students dancing, chatting, and laughing under the dim string lights, he couldn't help but feel a mix of curiosity and unease.

"First time at a hostel party?" a voice drawled from beside him.

Jinender turned to see a tall, lanky guy with messy hair and a cigarette dangling from his lips. He wore a faded band T-shirt and jeans with holes in the knees, and his eyes had a glazed, faraway look.

"Uh, yeah," Jinender replied, trying to sound casual.

The guy grinned, exhaling a cloud of smoke. "Relax, man. You'll get used to it. I'm Hitesh. Hitesh Tripathi."

"Jinender," he said, shaking Hitesh's hand.

Hitesh leaned against the wall, his posture relaxed, almost careless. "So, what's your story, Jinender? Freshman, right?"

"Yeah," Jinender said. "First year, Faculty of Law."

"Ah, a future lawyer," Hitesh said, his tone teasing. "Better enjoy life now before you're buried under case files and court dates."

Jinender chuckled nervously. "I guess."

Hitesh took a drag from his cigarette and glanced around the courtyard. "You know, college is the best time of your life. No rules, no responsibilities. Just you, your friends, and whatever makes you happy."

Jinender wasn't sure how to respond. Hitesh's carefree attitude was both intriguing and unsettling. He had never met anyone like him before.

"You smoke?" Hitesh asked, holding out a pack of cigarettes. "No, thanks," Jinender said quickly.

Hitesh shrugged. "Your loss. But if you ever want to try something... stronger, let me know. I know a guy."

Jinender's eyes widened. "Stronger?"

Hitesh laughed, a low, throaty sound. "Weed, man. It's not a big deal. Half the campus does it. It's not like we're hurting anyone. Just chilling, you know?"

Jinender didn't know. Back in Haryana, such things were unheard of–or at least, they were never talked about openly. But here, in this world of dim lights and loud music, it all seemed... normal.

"You should come hang out with us sometime," Hitesh said, pulling out his phone. "Here, give me your number. I'll show you around. Trust me, you'll love it."

Before Jinender could think twice, he found himself exchanging numbers with Hitesh.

Over the next few weeks, Jinender found himself drawn to Hitesh's world. It was so different from everything he had known–so free, so uninhibited. Hitesh introduced him to a group of seniors who spent their evenings smoking weed, listening to psychedelic music, and discussing philosophy. They talked about life, freedom, and the futility of societal norms, their words laced with a cynicism that Jinender found both fascinating and unsettling.

One evening, as they sat on the rooftop of the hostel, passing around a joint, Hitesh leaned back and said, "You know, Jinender, life's too short to worry about rules. Do what makes you happy. That's the only law that matters."

Jinender hesitated, the joint in his hand feeling heavier than it should. "But... isn't that kind of selfish? What about responsibilities? What about doing the right thing?"

Hitesh laughed. "The 'right thing'? Who decides what's right? Society? The government? Nah, man. You've got to live for yourself. That's the only way to be truly free."

Jinender didn't know what to say. Part of him admired Hitesh's confidence, his ability to live life on his own terms. But another part of him—the part that had grown up in a small town in Haryana, where values like hard work and discipline were ingrained—felt uneasy.

Still, he couldn't deny the thrill of it all. The secrecy, the rebellion, the sense of belonging to something bigger, something forbidden. It was intoxicating in a way he hadn't expected.

One night, as Jinender lay in his hostel bed, staring at the ceiling, his phone buzzed. It was a message from Hitesh.

"Hey, man. There's a guy near the back gate who's got some really good stuff. You in?"

Jinender stared at the screen, his heart racing. He knew he should say no. He knew this wasn't who he was. But the allure of the unfamiliar was too strong to resist.

"Yeah," he typed back. "I'm in."

As he slipped out of his room and into the night, Jinender couldn't shake the feeling that he was stepping into a new chapter of his life—one that was thrilling, dangerous, and utterly unpredictable.

And for the first time, he wasn't sure if he was ready for it.

Chapter 4: The Allure of the Forbidden

Delhi had a way of pulling Jinender Pratap Singh into its whirlwind of chaos and luxury. The city was a stark contrast to the quiet, disciplined life he had known in Haryana. Here, the nights were alive with neon lights, the air thick with the scent of street food and the hum of endless conversations. The more time Jinender spent with Hitesh Tripathi, the more he found himself drawn to this carefree, rebellious lifestyle. It was thrilling, intoxicating, and utterly foreign to him.

One evening, as they sat on the rooftop of the hostel, Hitesh leaned back against the wall, a cigarette dangling from his lips. The city skyline stretched out before them, a sea of lights and possibilities.

"You know," Hitesh said, his voice low and conspiratorial, "the stuff we get here in Delhi is garbage compared to what's out there."

Jinender raised an eyebrow. "What do you mean?"

Hitesh smirked, taking a drag from his cigarette. "My cousin, he's been traveling lately. Went to the northeast—Assam, Meghalaya, those parts. He got his hands on some of the best green hybrid stuff you can imagine. Pure, potent, and unlike anything you'll find in Delhi."

Jinender's curiosity was piqued. "And?"

"And," Hitesh continued, his eyes gleaming, "there's a huge demand for that kind of quality here. People would pay top dollar for it. We could make a killing."

Jinender's heart raced. The idea was risky, dangerous even, but the thought of easy money was undoubtedly alluring. He had never been one to break the rules, but the thrill of it all was hard to resist.

"But how would we even get it?" Jinender asked, trying to sound casual.

Hitesh leaned in closer, his voice dropping to a whisper. "That's where your friend comes in. Jia, right? She's from Shillong. If we can convince her to help us, we could get our hands on the good stuff without any hassle."

Jinender's stomach churned at the mention of Jia. She was sharp, principled, and fiercely independent. There was no way she would agree to something like this.

"Jia won't go for it," Jinender said quickly. "She's not that kind of person."

Hitesh shrugged, unfazed. "Then we don't tell her. We go to Shillong ourselves, grab what we need, and come back. Simple."

Jinender hesitated. The plan was reckless, but the more Hitesh talked, the more it made sense. They could make enough money to live comfortably, to enjoy the luxuries of Delhi without worrying about their next meal.

"How would we even get there?" Jinender asked.

Hitesh grinned. "Train routes. Cheap, discreet, and no one will suspect a thing. We'll go during the college break, make the trip, and be back before anyone even notices we're gone."

The idea was taking shape in Jinender's mind, and despite his reservations, he couldn't deny the thrill of it. It was a chance to break free from the monotony of his life, to step into the unknown and come out on top.

The days leading up to the college break were a blur of planning and anticipation. Jinender and Hitesh spent hours discussing the details–how much they would need, where they would store it, how they would distribute it. Hitesh's confidence was infectious, and Jinender found himself getting swept up in the excitement.

But there was a part of him that couldn't shake the guilt. He thought of Jia , of how she would react if she ever found out. She was his friend, someone he respected and admired. Betraying her trust felt wrong, but the allure of the plan was too strong to ignore.

The night before their departure, Jinender lay in his hostel bed, staring at the ceiling. His mind raced with thoughts of what lay ahead. He thought of his parents back in Haryana, of the values they had instilled in him. He thought of Jia , of her unwavering principles and fierce independence.

But then he thought of the money, the freedom, the thrill of it all.

The journey to Shillong was long and exhausting, but Jinender and Hitesh were too focused on their mission to care. They arrived in the early hours of the morning, the cool mountain air a stark contrast to the heat and chaos of Delhi.

Hitesh had arranged a meeting with a local contact through his cousin. The man was waiting for them at a small, dimly lit café on the outskirts of the city. He was older, with a weathered face and eyes that seemed to see right through them.

"You're the guys from Delhi?" the man asked, his voice low and gravelly.

Hitesh nodded, his usual confidence replaced with a rare sense of caution. "Yeah. We're here for the stuff."

The man studied them for a moment before nodding. "Follow me."

They drove to a secluded spot outside the city, where the man handed them a large, unmarked bag. Inside was the green hybrid stuff Hitesh had been raving about.

"This is the best you'll find," the man said. "Don't waste it."

Jinender's hands trembled as he took the bag. The weight of what they were doing hit him all at once. This wasn't just a reckless adventure anymore–it was real, and the consequences could be severe.

But there was no turning back now.

The train ride back to Delhi was tense. Jinender and Hitesh kept the bag hidden under their seats, their eyes darting around nervously at every stop. The thrill of the plan had been replaced with a gnawing sense of dread, but they were in too deep to back out.

As the train pulled into Delhi, Jinender felt a mix of relief and apprehension. They had done it. They had the stuff. Now all that was left was to distribute it and make the money.

But as they stepped off the train and into the chaos of the city, Jinender couldn't shake the feeling that they were playing with fire.

And sooner or later, they were going to get burned.

Chapter 5:
The Close Call

The money kept flowing, and so did the thrill. Jinender Pratap Singh and Hitesh Tripathi had built a small but lucrative operation, selling their premium stash to hostel students and a few select clients. The risks were high, but so were the rewards. Jinender had never imagined he'd be living this kind of life—parties, cash, and a sense of invincibility that came with every successful deal.

But the cracks were starting to show.

It all began when Hitesh's cousin connected them to an NLU Bangalore student who was willing to pay top dollar for their product. The catch? They had to courier it. Hitesh, always the risk-taker, was all in. Jinender, however, had reservations.

"This is too risky," Jinender argued one evening as they sat in their hostel room, counting cash. "What if the package gets intercepted?"

Hitesh waved him off, lighting a cigarette. "Relax, man. We'll use a fake consignee name. Even if something goes wrong, they won't trace it back to us."

Jinender wasn't convinced, but the promise of easy money silenced his doubts. They packed the parcel carefully, using a fake name and address for both the sender and receiver. Hitesh, wearing a blue hoodie with the University of Delhi logo, dropped it off at the courier service early one morning.

For a few days, everything seemed fine. Then, the news hit.

It was Rohan who first heard about it. He burst into their room one afternoon, his face pale.

"Guys, have you heard? NCB officials were at the hostel next door, asking about suspicious parcels. Someone said they're investigating a drug shipment."

Jinender's heart dropped. He exchanged a panicked glance with Hitesh, who was trying to look calm but failing miserably.

"What kind of parcels?" Jinender asked, his voice steady despite the fear gnawing at him.

"I don't know," Rohan said, shrugging. "But they're asking a lot of questions. People are freaking out."

Once Rohan left, Jinender turned to Hitesh, his anger bubbling to the surface. "This is your fault," he hissed. "I told you this was a bad idea!"

Hitesh shot him a glare. "My fault? You were in on it too, remember? Don't act like you're innocent."

Jinender clenched his fists, his mind racing. He knew they were in deep trouble. The fake consignee name might protect them for now, but if the NCB dug deeper, they could be caught.

Then came the real blow.

A few days later, rumours started circulating around campus. Someone had seen CCTV footage from the courier service. The footage showed a guy in a blue hoodie with the University of Delhi logo dropping off a suspicious package. His face was covered—thanks to the COVID mask mandate—but the hoodie was unmistakable.

Jinender's blood ran cold. He knew it was Hitesh.

"They're going to find us," Jinender said, pacing their room. "That hoodie is everywhere on campus. It's only a matter of time before someone connects the dots."

Hitesh, for once, looked shaken. "We'll figure it out," he said, though his voice lacked its usual confidence.

"Figure it out? How?" Jinender snapped. "This isn't some college prank, Hitesh. This is serious. We could go to jail."

The two of them argued late into the night, their voices low but sharp. Hitesh wanted to lay low and hope the NCB would move on. Jinender, however, knew they needed a smarter plan.

Jinender's mind was a whirlwind of thoughts. He couldn't let this ruin his life. He had worked too hard to get into law school, to build a future. He wasn't going to let it all go up in smoke because of one reckless decision.

"We need to destroy any evidence," Jinender said finally, his voice firm. "The leftover stash, the cash, everything. And we need to act normal. No more deals, no more parties. We pretend like nothing happened."

Hitesh hesitated. "What about the hoodie?"

Jinender paused, his mind racing. Then, an idea struck him—a risky but brilliant one.

"We're going to flood the campus with those hoodies," Jinender said, a determined glint in his eyes.

Hitesh frowned. "What do you mean?"

"We'll use the cash we've made to buy hundreds of those blue hoodies from different vendors around campus," Jinender explained. "Then, we'll anonymously gift them to as many students as possible. If half the campus is wearing the same hoodie, the NCB will never be able to connect the dots."

Hitesh's eyes widened, and then a slow grin spread across his face. "That's... actually genius."

Over the next few days, Jinender and Hitesh worked quietly but efficiently. They visited multiple vendors, purchasing blue hoodies with the University of Delhi logo in bulk. They made sure to spread out their purchases, avoiding any suspicion.

Once they had enough hoodies, they began their next phase. Late at night, they would leave the hoodies outside random hostel rooms, in common areas, and even in lecture halls. They included anonymous notes: "A gift from a fellow student. Stay warm!"

The plan worked better than they could have imagined. Within a week, the blue hoodie became a campus trend. Students wore them to classes, to the canteen, and even to parties. The hoodie was everywhere.

When the NCB officials returned to campus, they were met with a sea of blue hoodies. Everywhere they looked, students were wearing the same logo, the same color. The CCTV footage, which had once seemed like a breakthrough, was now useless.

Jinender watched from a distance as the officials grew increasingly frustrated. They questioned a few students, but with no clear suspect and no way to narrow down their search, they were forced to move on.

That night, Jinender and Hitesh sat on the rooftop, the city lights stretching out before them. For the first time in weeks, Jinender felt a sense of relief.

"We did it," Hitesh said, lighting a cigarette. "We actually pulled it off."

Jinender nodded, but his relief was tinged with guilt. He had outsmarted the NCB, but at what cost? The thrill of the game was fading, replaced by the weight of what they had done.

"This has to stop," Jinender said quietly. "No more deals, no more risks. We're done."

Hitesh looked at him, his expression unreadable. For a moment, Jinender thought he might argue. But then Hitesh simply nodded.

"Yeah," he said, exhaling a cloud of smoke. "We're done."

As Jinender stared out at the city, he couldn't shake the feeling that this was only the beginning of the consequences. The NCB might have been fooled, but the choices they had made would haunt them for a long time.

And Jinender knew one thing for sure–he never wanted to live like this again.

Chapter 6: The Net Tightens the NCB wasn't Giving Up.

Jinender Pratap Singh had hoped their clever plan with the hoodies would throw the officials off their trail, but the Narcotics Control Bureau was more determined than ever. They had started digging deeper, piecing together every tiny clue they could find. The fake consignee and consigner details, the hoodie, the unusual quality of the substance–it all pointed to something bigger, something more organized.

Jinender, meanwhile, was trying to move on. The close call with the NCB had shaken him to his core. He had seen how quickly things could spiral out of control, how one reckless decision could destroy everything he had worked for. He had made a promise to himself: no more risks, no more illegal schemes. It was time to focus on what really mattered–his studies and his future.

He threw himself into his classes, determined to make up for the time he had lost. The upcoming KK luthra moot court competition was his new obsession. It was a chance to prove himself, to show that he was more than just a guy who got caught up in a dangerous game.

But the past wasn't ready to let him go.

The NCB's investigation was gaining momentum. They had analyzed the substance in the intercepted package and found something unusual–it wasn't the typical low-grade stuff commonly found in Delhi. This was fresh, high-quality, and likely sourced from a high- altitude region.

"This isn't local," one of the NCB officers said during a briefing. "It's from the northeast. Probably Meghalaya or Assam. Whoever sent this has connections there."

The officers began cross-referencing travel records, looking for anyone who had recently traveled to the northeast. They also noticed a pattern–the fake consignee and consigner addresses were both located near the hostels where law students resided.

"It's possible we're dealing with a student," the lead investigator said. "Someone who's either from the northeast or has travelled there recently. Let's narrow our search to the law faculty hostels."

Jinender, unaware of how close the NCB was getting, was busy preparing for the moot court competition. He spent hours in the library, researching case laws and drafting arguments. Jia, who was also participating, had become his study partner.

"You've changed," Jia remarked one evening as they sat in the library. "You're more focused. What happened?"

Jinender hesitated. He wanted to tell her everything–about Hitesh, about the NCB, about the guilt that kept him awake at night. But he couldn't. Not yet.

"I just realized I was wasting my time," he said finally. "I want to be a good lawyer. Maybe even a great one. I can't do that if I'm distracted."

Jia smiled. "I'm glad to hear that. You've got potential, Jinender. Don't waste it."

Meanwhile, Hitesh was growing restless. The NCB's increased activity had him on edge, and he didn't share Jinender's newfound determination to stay clean.

"We're sitting on a goldmine," Hitesh argued one night as they sat in their room. "We can't just walk away because of a little heat."

"A little heat?" Jinender snapped. "The NCB is crawling all over campus, Hitesh. They're not going to stop until they find someone. And if they connect the dots, it's over for us."

Hitesh leaned back, his expression defiant. "We've been careful. They've got nothing on us."

"They've got enough," Jinender said, his voice low. "The hoodie, the travel records, the fake addresses–it's only a matter of time before they figure it out."

Hitesh didn't respond, but Jinender could see the doubt in his eyes.

The NCB's investigation took a new turn when they received a tip from a secret source. The source claimed that the substance in the package was fresh and likely sourced directly from the northeast. They also mentioned that the person behind it had traveled to the region recently.

The officers began cross-referencing travel records with student databases. They focused on law students, particularly those with connections to the northeast or recent travel history.

Jinender was in the middle of a moot court practice session when he heard the news. Rohan burst into the room, his face pale.

"The NCB is questioning North Eastern Students," Rohan said, his voice urgent. "They think someone is involved in some drug case."

Jinender's heart dropped. He knew that Jia had nothing to do with their operation, but the NCB's interest in North East Student was a dangerous sign. If they started digging into, they might uncover the truth.

"We need to do something," Jinender said, his mind racing.

Hitesh, who had been lounging in the corner, looked up. "Like what? Turn ourselves in?"

"No," Jinender said firmly. "We need to make sure No innocent doesn't get dragged into this. And we need to cover our tracks—for good this time.

As the NCB closed in, Jinender realized the stakes were higher than ever. He had started this journey chasing money and thrills, but now he was fighting to protect his friends and his future.

The net was tightening, and Jinender knew he had to stay one step ahead. But with every move he made, the risks grew greater.

And the NCB wasn't the only threat. Hitesh's recklessness was becoming a liability, and Jinender wasn't sure how much longer he could keep things under control.

The game was far from over, and the consequences were just beginning.

Chapter 7: Bait the Hunters

The weight of the situation pressed heavily on Jinender Pratap Singh's shoulders. Hitesh's carefree attitude and reckless decisions had brought them to the brink of disaster, and Jinender knew he could no longer rely on him. The NCB was closing in, and if they didn't act soon, both of them would be caught. Jinender realized that the only way out of this mess was to outsmart the hunters–the NCB itself. But to do that, he needed to understand the rules of the game.

Jinender spent the next week buried in research. He pored over the Narcotic Drugs and Psychotropic Substances (NDPS) Act, studying its provisions, loopholes, and the procedures followed by the NCB during investigations. He read through countless judgments, analysing how courts interpreted the law and how the NCB built its cases. He learned about the importance of evidence chains, the role of informants, and the legal thresholds required for arrests and convictions. The more he read, the more he realized that the NCB's strength lay in its ability to connect dots—dots that Jinender needed to scatter.

Hitesh, oblivious to the gravity of the situation, continued to brush off Jinender's concerns. "Relax, man," he said one evening, lounging on his bed with a cigarette. "They've got nothing on us. We're too smart for them."

Jinender snapped. "You don't get it, Hitesh! This isn't some college prank. If they catch us, we're looking at years in prison. Do you understand that? Years. And I'm not going down because of your carelessness."

Hitesh raised an eyebrow, clearly taken aback by Jinender's outburst. "Okay, okay. What's your plan, then?"

Jinender took a deep breath. "I'm going to bait them. If we can't stop the investigation, we'll redirect it. But I need you to stay out of this. No more deals, no more risks. Just lay low."

Hitesh shrugged, clearly unconvinced. "Whatever you say, boss."

Jinender's plan was risky, but it was the only way he could think of to throw the NCB off their trail. He needed to create a diversion, something that would make the investigators question their assumptions. And to do that, he needed to exploit their biases.

He started by researching areas in Delhi with a high concentration of North Eastern residents. He knew the NCB was already fixated on the northeast connection due to the quality of the substance they had intercepted. If he could plant a false lead that pointed to someone from the region, it might buy them enough time to cover their tracks.

After days of careful planning, Jinender finalized his strategy. He would send an anonymous tip to the NCB, using a cyber café in a North Eastern-dominated area. The tip would suggest that the intercepted package was part of a larger network operating from Manipur. To make it convincing, he would use a fake North Eastern name and a VPN to mask his location.

The day of the operation arrived. Jinender spent hours preparing, ensuring every detail was perfect. He changed his appearance as much as possible—cutting his hair shorter, wearing glasses he didn't need, and dressing in a hoodie and mask to obscure his face. He even practiced walking with a slight limp to further disguise himself.

He chose a cyber café in Humayunpur, a neighborhood known for its North Eastern population. The café was small and dimly lit, with rows of outdated computers and a bored attendant at the counter. Jinender paid in cash, using a fake name to register. He chose a computer in the corner, away from prying eyes.

Once logged in, he activated a VPN, setting his virtual location to Manipur. He created a new email account using a generic North Eastern-sounding name—Ramesh Meitei—and drafted the tip carefully. The email claimed that the intercepted package was part of a larger operation run by a Manipur-based syndicate. It provided vague but plausible details, enough to pique the NCB's interest without giving away too much.

Jinender hesitated for a moment before hitting send. This was the point of no return. If the NCB traced the email back to him, it would be game over. But if it worked, it could buy them the time they needed.

He clicked send, deleted the email account, and cleared the browser history. As he left the café, he felt a mix of relief and dread. The plan was in motion, but the stakes were higher than ever.

The next few days were tense. Jinender kept a low profile, avoiding Hitesh and focusing on his studies. He monitored the news, waiting for any sign that the NCB had taken the bait.

Then, it happened. A week after sending the email, Jinender saw a news article about the NCB expanding its investigation to include potential links to Manipur. The article mentioned that the agency was following up on a tip about a syndicate operating in the region. Jinender felt a surge of hope—his plan was working.

But the relief was short-lived. The NCB wasn't giving up on their original lead. They continued to question students, particularly those with connections to the northeast. Jinender realized that his diversion had bought them some time, but it wasn't enough. He needed to do more.

The NCB's focus on Manipur had bought Jinender some much-needed time, but he wasn't naive enough to think it was over. The hunters were still out there, and they were relentless. He knew the NCB wouldn't stop until they had someone to pin the case on, and if they ever connected the dots back to him and Hitesh, it would be game over. Jinender couldn't afford to let his guard down. He had to prepare for the worst.

One evening, Jinender met Hitesh in a secluded corner of the campus. Hitesh looked more subdued than usual, the weight of the situation finally starting to sink in. Jinender didn't waste time with small talk.

"We're not out of the woods yet," Jinender said, his voice low but urgent. "The NCB might be chasing the Manipur lead for now, but they'll come back to us eventually. We need to make sure there's nothing left for them to find."

Hitesh frowned. "What do you mean? We've already covered our tracks with the hoodies and the fake tip. What else is there?"

Jinender leaned in closer, his tone serious. "Digital footprints, Hitesh. If the NCB seizes our phones or laptops, their digital forensics team will tear them apart. They'll find everything– our search history, our travel records, our messages. And once they have that, it's over."

Hitesh's eyes widened as the realization hit him. "Shit. I didn't think about that."

"Exactly," Jinender said. "That's why we need to wipe everything clean. Every search, every message, every photo–

anything that could link us to the northeast or the parcel. We need to make it look like we were never involved."

Hitesh nodded, his usual carefree demeanor replaced by a rare sense of focus. "Okay. What do we do?"

Jinender had spent hours researching how to erase digital footprints. He knew it wasn't as simple as deleting files or clearing browser history. The NCB's digital forensics team could recover almost anything if they had the right tools. He needed to ensure that every trace of their involvement was gone for good.

First, they started with their phones. Jinender walked Hitesh through the process of factory resetting their devices, ensuring that all data was permanently erased. They removed SIM cards and memory cards, destroying them to eliminate any chance of recovery.

Next, they moved on to their laptops. Jinender used a secure data-wiping software to overwrite the hard drives multiple times, making it nearly impossible for anyone to retrieve deleted files. He also cleared their browsing history, cookies, and cached data, ensuring there was no trace of their online activity.

"What about our travel records?" Hitesh asked, his voice tinged with anxiety. "We booked those train tickets online. What if the NCB finds out?"

Jinender had already thought of that. He accessed their email accounts and deleted all records of their train bookings to the northeast. He also cleared their search history related to the trip, including any maps or travel guides they had looked up.

"We need to be thorough," Jinender said, his fingers flying across the keyboard. "Even the smallest detail could give us away."

Once their devices were clean, Jinender turned his attention to their online presence. He knew the NCB could subpoena social media platforms for their data, so he took extra precautions. He deactivated their social media accounts, deleting all posts, messages, and photos that could be used against them. He even went as far as creating fake accounts with generic names to muddy the waters.

"What about the cyber café?" Hitesh asked, his voice barely above a whisper. "You sent that email from there. What if they trace it back to you?"

Jinender had anticipated this. "I used a VPN to mask my location, and I paid in cash with a fake name. The café's CCTV footage is grainy, and I made sure to disguise myself. Even if they find the café, they won't be able to identify me."

Hitesh looked impressed. "You've thought of everything, haven't you?"

"I had to," Jinender replied, his tone grim. "This isn't just about us anymore. If we get caught, it's not just our futures that are ruined. Our families, our friends–they'll all suffer too."

As the night wore on, Jinender and Hitesh worked tirelessly to eliminate every possible link to their operation. By the time they were done, the first rays of sunlight were peeking through the windows. Jinender leaned back in his chair, exhausted but satisfied.

"We've done all we can," he said, rubbing his eyes. "But we can't let our guard down. The NCB is still out there, and they're not going to stop until they find someone to blame."

Hitesh nodded, his usual bravado replaced by a quiet determination. "I get it now. This is serious. I'll lay low, no more risks."

Jinender studied his friend for a moment, relieved to see that Hitesh finally understood the stakes. "Good. Because if we slip up now, everything we've done will be for nothing."

The days that followed were tense. Jinender kept a close eye on the news, watching for any updates on the NCB's investigation. The agency's focus on Manipur continued, but Jinender knew it was only a matter of time before they circled back to Delhi.

He spent his free time studying the NDPS Act and court judgments, preparing for the worst. He knew that if they were caught, their only hope would be to fight the case in court. And to do that, he needed to understand the law inside and out.

One evening, as he sat in the library, Jia approached him. She had been distant since Hitesh's arrest, but Jinender could tell she was worried.

"You look like you haven't slept in days," she said, sitting down across from him. "What's going on, Jinender?"

Jinender hesitated, torn between the need to confide in someone and the fear of dragging Jia into his mess. "It's complicated," he said finally. "But I'm handling it. I just need to stay focused."

Jia studied him for a moment, her expression softening. "You don't have to do this alone, you know. Whatever it is, I'm here for you."

Jinender felt a lump in his throat. He wanted to tell her everything, to unburden himself of the guilt and fear that had been weighing him down. But he couldn't. Not yet.

"Thanks, Jia ," he said quietly. "That means a lot."

As the weeks passed, Jinender continued to prepare for the worst. He knew the NCB wouldn't stop until they had someone to blame, and he was determined to make sure it wasn't him or Hitesh. He had started this journey chasing money and thrills, but now he was fighting for his future—and for the people he cared about.

The hunters were still out there, closing in with every passing day. But Jinender was ready. He had baited them, diverted their attention, and erased every trace of his involvement. Now, all he could do was wait and watch, knowing that the game was far from over.

And when the time came, Jinender Pratap Singh would be ready to face the hunters head-on, it reminded him of a quote of a criminal defence lawyer, namely N.P Singh, **"The law best also know how to bend it.**

Chapter 8: Summer Shadows and New Beginnings

The summer break brought a wave of change to the Faculty of Law. As the campus emptied out, students packed their bags and headed home, leaving the once-bustling corridors eerily quiet. For the NCB, this was bad news. Their investigation, which had already hit a dead end, was further hampered by the absence of key suspects—particularly the North Eastern students who had returned to their hometowns. With no fresh leads and dwindling interest, the case began to lose momentum. For Jinender Pratap Singh, this was a welcome relief, but he knew better than to let his guard down completely.

Jinender had grown distant from Hitesh over the past few weeks. The close call with the NCB had been a wake-up call, and Jinender realized that Hitesh's reckless behavior was a liability he could no longer afford. While Hitesh remained his friend, Jinender made a conscious decision to limit their interactions. He had learned his lesson the hard way, and he wasn't about to risk everything again.

Instead, Jinender found himself spending more time with Jia . Both of them had decided to stay back in Delhi during the summer break, opting to intern under a Senior Advocate rather than returning home. The internship was a golden opportunity to gain practical experience in criminal law, and Jinender was determined to make the most of it. Little did he know, this summer would change his life in ways he hadn't anticipated.

The internship was intense but rewarding. Jinender and Jia worked under Senior Advocate Rehmat Mir, a seasoned criminal lawyer known for his sharp mind and no-nonsense approach. The days were long, filled with drafting petitions, researching case laws, and attending court hearings. But Jinender thrived in the fast-paced environment, soaking up every bit of knowledge like a sponge.

Jia , too, was in her element. Her passion for human rights and criminal justice shone through in her work, and Jinender couldn't help but admire her dedication. They made a great team, often brainstorming arguments for cases late into the evening. But it wasn't all work. After a long day at the office, they would unwind at their favorite spot—a small Chinese restaurant called Shagun, tucked away in a quiet corner of Kamla Nagar.

Shagun was a modest place, with red lanterns hanging from the ceiling and the aroma of steamed momos filling the air. It had become their go-to spot, partly because of Jia's love for momos and partly because it was one of the few places where they could relax without the weight of their responsibilities. Over plates of spicy chicken momos and cups of steaming chai, they would talk about everything—law, life, and their dreams for the future.

One evening, as they sat at their usual table, Jia looked at Jinender with a playful smile. "You know, I never thought I'd find someone who loves momos as much as I do."

Jinender laughed. "What can I say? You've converted me. I used to be a samosa guy, but these momos are something else."

Jia 's smile softened, and for a moment, there was a quiet understanding between them. The kind of understanding that comes from shared experiences and late-night conversations. Jinender felt a warmth in his chest, a feeling he hadn't experienced in a long time.

"You've changed, Jinender," Jia said, her voice gentle. "You're more focused, more driven. I like this version of you."

Jinender looked at her, his heart skipping a beat. "I guess I've had a lot of time to think. And being around you... it's made me want to be better."

Jia's cheeks flushed, and she looked down at her plate. "You're already pretty great, you know."

The air between them was charged with unspoken emotions. Jinender reached across the table, his hand brushing against hers. "Jia , I—"

Before he could finish, the waiter arrived with their bill, breaking the moment. Jia quickly pulled her hand away, her face still flushed. "We should probably head back. Early day tomorrow."

Jinender nodded, though his mind was still reeling from what had just happened. As they walked back to their hostel, the silence between them was comfortable, yet filled with possibilities.

The days turned into weeks, and Jinender and Jia grew closer. They spent their evenings exploring Delhi, discovering hidden gems like the bustling lanes of Majnu Ka Tila, the serene Lodhi Gardens, and the vibrant Dilli Haat. Each outing brought them closer, their bond deepening with every shared laugh and stolen glance.

But amidst the newfound warmth in his life, Jinender couldn't shake the feeling that something was off. He hadn't seen Hitesh in weeks, and while that was partly by design, he couldn't help but worry. Hitesh had always been unpredictable, and Jinender knew better than to assume he had changed his ways.

His fears were confirmed one evening when he ran into Hitesh near the hostel. Hitesh looked dishevelled, his eyes bloodshot and his demeanor restless.

"Jinender, my man!" Hitesh said, clapping him on the back. "Long time no see. How's the internship going?"

Jinender forced a smile. "It's going well. What about you? What have you been up to?" Hitesh's grin turned sly. "Oh, you know. Just planning my next big move."

Jinender's stomach dropped. "What kind of move?"

Hitesh leaned in closer, lowering his voice. "I've got a new connection. Malana cream, straight from Himachal. Top quality, and there's a huge demand for it on campus. This could be our chance to make some real money."

Jinender's heart sank. "Hitesh, are you serious? After everything that happened? You're going to risk it all again?"

Hitesh shrugged, his expression defiant. "A leopard can't change its spots, Jinender. This is who I am. And besides, I've learned from my mistakes. This time, I'll be smarter."

Jinender shook his head, a mix of anger and disappointment bubbling inside him. "You're playing with fire, Hitesh. And when you get burned, don't come crying to me."

Hitesh's smile faded, replaced by a look of resentment. "Fine. Stay in your little bubble. But don't blame me when you're stuck in some boring corporate job while I'm living the high life."

Jinender watched as Hitesh walked away, his heart heavy. He knew there was no stopping him. Hitesh was determined to walk down this path, no matter the consequences.

As Jinender made his way back to his room, he couldn't shake the feeling of dread. Hitesh's recklessness was a ticking time bomb, and Jinender knew it was only a matter of time before it exploded. But for now, he had to focus on what mattered–his internship, his future, and the growing connection with Jia .

The summer had brought new beginnings, but it had also cast long shadows. And as Jinender lay in bed that night, he couldn't help but wonder how long it would be before those shadows caught up with him.

Chapter 9:
The Final Stretch

The final semester at the Faculty of Law was a whirlwind of emotions. The once-daunting journey was now nearing its end, and Jinender Pratap Singh couldn't help but feel a mix of nostalgia and anticipation. The campus, with its red-brick buildings and sprawling lawns, had become a second home. The North Campus area, with its vibrant energy and endless possibilities, was a place where dreams were forged and memories were made. From the bustling streets of Kamla Nagar to the serene corners of Arts Faculty, every corner of the campus held a story.

Jinender, Jia , Rohan, and Aryan were now in the final stretch of their law school journey. The pressure was mounting as they prepared for mock trials, practical subjects, and their final exams. Each of them had their own aspirations and plans for the future, and the reality of leaving behind the comfort of college life was beginning to sink in.

Jia had always been passionate about human rights and social justice, but her internship experience had steered her in a new direction. The practical exposure to criminal law had ignited a desire to pursue a career in the judiciary. She spent hours poring over study material for the judicial services exam, her determination unwavering.

"I want to make a difference," she told Jinender one evening as they sat in the Faculty canteen. "Not just through activism, but by being in a position where I can bring about real change."

Jinender admired her focus and drive. "You'll make an amazing judge, Jia . I have no doubt about it."

Jia smiled, her eyes sparkling with determination. "What about you, Jinender? What's your plan after graduation?"

Jinender hesitated. He had been so caught up in the present that he hadn't given much thought to the future. "I'm not sure yet. Maybe litigation, or corporate law. I just know I want to make the most of whatever comes my way."

Rohan, the quiet and hardworking one, had his sights set on higher education. He had applied for a master's program at King's College London, and the acceptance letter had arrived just a week ago. His dream of specializing in international law was finally within reach.

"London, here I come!" Rohan said, waving the acceptance letter in the air. "I can't believe this is actually happening."

Aryan, ever the smooth talker, had a different plan. "Corporate life for me," he declared. "I've already got a few offers lined up. Let's see which one pays the most."

Jinender laughed. "Of course, that's your priority."

Despite their different paths, the four friends were united by their shared goal of scoring at least 60% in their final exams–a challenging feat in the rigorous academic environment of the University of Delhi. They spent countless hours in the library, poring over case laws and drafting arguments for their mock trials. The pressure was intense, but it was also a time of bonding and camaraderie.

One evening, as they sat on the steps of the Faculty building, watching the sun set over the campus, Jinender felt a wave of nostalgia. "I can't believe we're almost done," he said. "It feels like just yesterday we were freshmen, trying to figure out where the lecture halls were."

Jia nodded, her expression wistful. "Time flies. But we've made some amazing memories, haven't we?"

"We sure have," Aryan said, grinning. "From late-night chai at Shagun to those endless debates in the canteen, this place has been our playground."

Rohan smiled. "And soon, we'll be out there in the real world, chasing our dreams."

Jinender looked at Jia , his heart swelling with emotions he had been trying to suppress. Over the past few months, his feelings for her had grown stronger, but he had never found the right moment to confess. Every time he tried, he would chicken out, unsure of how she would react.

"Jia ," he began, his voice trembling slightly. "There's something I've been meaning to tell you."

Jia turned to him, her eyes curious. "What is it?"

Jinender opened his mouth to speak, but the words caught in his throat. "I… I just wanted to say that I'm really glad we became friends. You've been such an important part of my journey here."

Jia smiled, though there was a hint of disappointment in her eyes. "I'm glad too, Jinender. You're one of the best friends I've ever had."

Jinender's heart sank. He had missed his chance–again.

Life went on, and the group continued to make the most of their final days in college. They explored every corner of North Campus, from the iconic Vishwavidyalaya Metro Station to the bustling streets of Hudson Lane. They spent evenings at Kamla Nagar Market, indulging in street food and shopping for souvenirs. They even made a trip to Majnu Ka Tila, the Tibetan colony, where they gorged on momos and thukpa, reminiscing about their college days.

But amidst the laughter and camaraderie, Jinender couldn't shake the feeling that something was off. He hadn't heard from Hitesh in months, and while he had initially been relieved, he now felt a growing sense of unease. Hitesh's absence was like a dark cloud hanging over him, a reminder of the past he had tried so hard to leave behind.

One evening, as Jinender was preparing for his mock trial, his phone buzzed. It was an unknown number. He hesitated for a moment before answering.

"Hello?" he said cautiously.

"Is this Jinender Pratap Singh?" a stern voice asked on the other end. "Yes, speaking. Who is this?"

"This is Officer Sharma from the Narcotics Control Bureau. We're trying to locate Hitesh Tripathi. Do you know his current whereabouts?"

Jinender's heart skipped a beat. His mind raced as he tried to process the question. "I... I haven't seen or spoken to Hitesh in months. Why are you looking for him?"

There was a pause on the other end. "We need to speak with him regarding an ongoing investigation. If you have any information, it would be in your best interest to cooperate."

Jinender's hands trembled as he ended the call. His mind was a whirlwind of thoughts. What had Hitesh done now? And why was the NCB involved again?

He tried calling Hitesh, but the number was unreachable. Panic set in as he realized that Hitesh's recklessness had finally caught up with him–and this time, there was no easy way out.

As Jinender sat in his room, staring at his phone, he felt a sense of dread wash over him. The past he had tried so hard to escape was coming back to haunt him. He knew he had to find Hitesh before the NCB did, but he also knew that getting involved again could jeopardize everything he had worked for.

The final stretch of college was supposed to be a time of celebration and new beginnings. But for Jinender, it was turning into a race against time–a race to save his friend and, ultimately, himself.

Chapter 10: The Circle Closes

The final exams at the Faculty of Law were a blur of late-night study sessions, endless revisions, and the occasional nervous breakdown. Jinender Pratap Singh, despite the lingering worry about Hitesh, managed to stay focused. He knew this was his chance to close this chapter of his life on a high note. Alongside Jia, Rohan, and Aryan, he poured his heart into the exams, determined to make the most of the opportunity.

When the results were announced, it was a moment of triumph for all four friends. Jinender had scored well enough to enroll himself in the Bar Council of Delhi, fulfilling his dream of becoming an advocate. Jia , ever the perfectionist, had secured a distinction and was now preparing for the Delhi Judiciary exams. Rohan had received his acceptance to King's College London, and Aryan had landed a lucrative corporate job. Their paths diverged, but the bond they had forged over the years remained unshaken.

Yet, amidst the celebrations, there was an unspoken void. Hitesh was still missing, and no one had heard from him in months. Jinender had tried to push the thought aside, but the worry gnawed at him. He had no idea where Hitesh was or what he had been up to, and the uncertainty was unsettling.

Life moved on. Jinender joined the chamber of a seasoned trial lawyer at Tis Hazari Court, immersing himself in the practicalities of litigation. The bustling corridors of the court, the heated arguments, and the thrill of fighting for justice–it was everything he had dreamed of. But even as he settled into his new role, the shadow of Hitesh's absence loomed large.

One evening, as Jinender was preparing for a case, his phone buzzed. It was an anonymous number. He hesitated for a moment before answering.

"Hello?" he said cautiously.

" Hitesh ko NCB ne arrest kar liya hai," a heavy, trembling voice said on the other end. It was Hitesh's father Ayush.

Jinender's heart sank. "Uncle, what happened? Where is he?"

"He's in Rohini Jail No. 10. They arrested him yesterday. Beta, please help him. You're a lawyer now. You're his only hope."

Jinender assured Hitesh's father that he would do everything in his power to help. As he ended the call, his mind raced. He needed to see Hitesh, to understand what had happened.

The next morning, Jinender made his way to Rohini Jail. The sight of the high walls and barbed wire sent a chill down his spine. After completing the formalities, he was led to a small visitation room. Moments later, Hitesh was brought in, handcuffed and looking visibly shaken.

"Jinender," Hitesh said, his voice breaking as tears streamed down his face. "I messed up. I messed up big time."

Jinender took a deep breath, pushing aside his emotions. "What happened, Hitesh? Tell me everything."

Hitesh wiped his tears and began to explain. "After we stopped talking, I got greedy. I thought I could make one last big score. I started dealing with Malana cream hash again. I even tried to send a parcel to Amsterdam. But the NCB intercepted it. They've been after me for months. I've been on the run, but they finally caught me."

Jinender's jaw tightened. "And the previous case? The northeast connection? Do they know about that?"

Hitesh shook his head. "No, this is a separate case. They don't know anything about the past."

Jinender felt a wave of relief. At least they weren't digging into the old case. But the situation was still dire. Hitesh was facing serious charges, and the evidence against him seemed strong.

"I'll defend you," Jinender said firmly. "But you need to be honest with me. Every detail matters."

Hitesh nodded, his expression a mix of gratitude and guilt. "I'll tell you everything. Just... please don't give up on me."

It was an uphill battle, but Jinender was determined to give it his all.

One afternoon, he visited the NCB office at RK Puram to meet the Investigating Officer (IO) handling Hitesh's case. The IO, a stern-looking man in his forties, greeted him with a knowing smile.

"So, you're Hitesh Tripathi's lawyer," the IO said, leaning back in his chair. "I've heard about you. Fresh out of law school, aren't you?"

Jinender smiled politely, refusing to be intimidated. "Yes, sir. But I believe in justice, and I'm here to ensure my client gets a fair trial."

The IO chuckled. "Fair trial? Your client was caught red-handed with a parcel of hash destined for Amsterdam. The evidence is solid. What's there to defend?"

Jinender leaned forward, his tone calm but firm. "Evidence can be misleading, sir. And until it's proven beyond a reasonable doubt in a court of law, my client is innocent."

The IO raised an eyebrow, clearly amused. "You've got guts, kid. But let me tell you something—we know he did it. We've got everything we need to put him away for a long time."

Jinender met his gaze, unflinching. "Then you better prove it, sir. Because until you do, I'll be fighting for his freedom every step of the way."

The IO laughed, a deep, hearty laugh. "I like you, kid. You've got fire. But don't think for a second that this will be easy."

Jinender stood up, extending his hand. "I wouldn't have it any other way, sir."

As Jinender left the NCB office, he felt a surge of determination. The road ahead would be tough, but he was ready for the challenge. He had come a long way from the scared, uncertain freshman who had first stepped into the Faculty of Law. He was now an advocate, fighting for justice and standing up for what he believed in.

The circle had closed. The past had come back to haunt him, but Jinender was no longer running from it. He was facing it head-on, armed with the knowledge and skills he had gained over the years.

And as he walked away from the NCB office, he knew one thing for sure—this was just the beginning of his journey. The game was far from over, and Jinender Pratap Singh was ready to play it like a pro.

A criminal lawyer doesn't break the law—just finds the user manual the lawmakers forgot to read.

~Naerender Singh